PONY PALS

Magic Pony

Jeanne Betancourt

Illustrated by Paul Bachem

A
LITTLE APPLE
PAPERBACK

SCHOLASTIC INC.

New York   Toronto   London   Auckland   Sydney
Mexico City   New Delhi   Hong Kong   Buenos Aires

For Maria Barbo, editor and Pony Pal

ISBN 0-439-30645-0

12 11 10 9 8 7 6 5 4 3 2 1   2 3 4 5 6 7/0

Printed in the U.S.A.   40
First Scholastic printing, May 2002

Contents

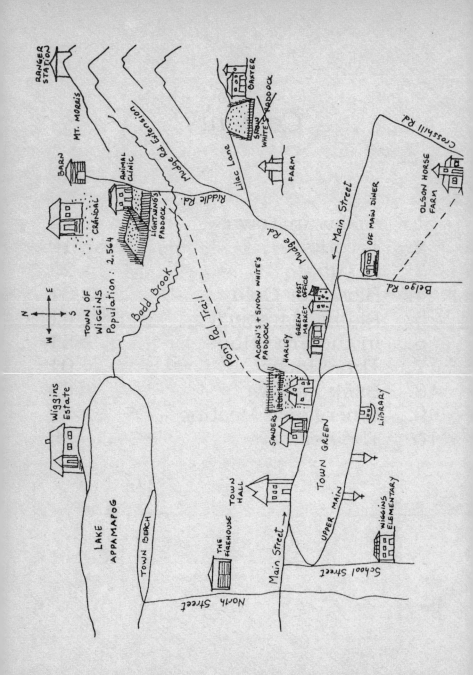

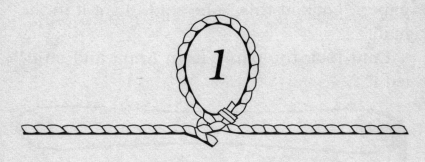

A Play in Town

Anna Harley ran to the paddock behind her house. Her Pony Pal Lulu was already in the paddock saddling up her pony, Snow White.

Anna climbed over the fence. "Come on, Acorn," she called to her pony. "We're going for a trail ride." Anna's Shetland pony, Acorn, flicked his tail and ran in the other direction.

"Acorn loves to play chase." Lulu laughed as she put the saddle on Snow White's back.

Anna handed Lulu a folded piece of yellow paper. "Look at this," she said. "I got it in the mail."

Lulu took the paper from Anna and studied it.

CASTING CALL

A WIGGINS PLAYERS PRODUCTION

MAGIC PONY

A PLAY FOR CHILDREN
WRITTEN AND DIRECTED BY WILLIAM PRENTICE

TRY OUT FOR A ROLE IN MAGIC PONY

WHO? 10- TO 12-YEAR-OLD GIRLS

10- TO 12-YEAR-OLD BOYS

PONIES

WHERE? LIBRARY PARK

WHEN? SATURDAY, 10 A.M.

"They need a pony for their play!" exclaimed Lulu. "Acorn should try out. He's such a good actor. You should try out, too, Anna. You'd get to be in a play with your pony."

Anna thought about being in a play. Actors had to memorize their lines. Anna didn't think she could do that.

"Acorn can try out," Anna said. "But I don't want to be in a play." She looked at her watch. "We had better hurry or we'll be late."

The two girls finished saddling up their ponies and rode onto Pony Pal Trail. The mile-and-a-half woodland trail connected Acorn and Snow White's paddock with Anna and Lulu's other Pony Pal, Pam Crandal's property. It was a perfect shortcut for the three friends.

Pam and Lightning were waiting for Anna and Lulu at the three birch trees. "There's going to be a play," Pam announced. "My mom told me. And there's a part for a pony."

"We know," said Anna and Lulu in unison.

"Let's ride to the brook and talk about it," suggested Pam. She turned Lightning around and led the way.

When they reached the brook, the ponies drank from the water. The girls sat on rocks and skipped stones.

"I wonder what a play called *Magic Pony* is about," said Lulu.

"Maybe it's about a pony that can do magic tricks," said Anna.

"Acorn knows a lot of tricks already," said Pam. "He should try out for the part." She skipped a stone across the water. It bounced three times.

Lulu's stone skipped twice. "Remember how great Acorn was in the circus?" she said. "He wasn't afraid of the noisy crowds and he nodded on command."

"And in the movie," added Pam, "he bowed and did whatever the director wanted."

"Acorn can try out," said Anna as she turned a smooth stone over in her hands.

"You should try out, too, Anna," said Pam.

"You're a good actor," added Lulu. "Remember when you pretended you wanted to buy a pony? That helped us save Cloud from a mean owner. Maggie the Magician believed you."

"I made up my own words for that," said Anna. She flicked a small, flat stone onto the water. It sank without skipping. "That's different from being in a play. In a play, you act out other people's words."

"I bet you can act other people's words, too," said Lulu.

Pam skipped another stone. It bounced three times. "I have an idea, Anna," she said. "I'll write a scene right now and you can act it. It'll be a test to see if you can act in a play."

"That's a great idea," said Lulu.

"There will be two parts in the scene," continued Pam. She took a small notebook and a pen out of her backpack. "Lulu, there'll be a part for you, too."

"Okay," agreed Lulu. "What's the play going to be about?"

Pam looked up at the sky and thought for a minute. "The main character is a girl who wants a pony," she said. "The other character is — her mother. That's you, Lulu."

Lulu smiled at Anna. "I'm going to be your *mother*," she teased.

While Pam wrote the scene, Lulu practiced skipping stones. Anna made a spiral design with small stones on a big, flat rock. The ponies grazed on the grass at the edge of the brook.

When Pam finished, she handed Anna the notebook. Anna and Lulu silently read over their parts.

"That's a really good scene," Lulu told Pam. "I can't believe you wrote it in ten minutes."

"Thanks," said Pam. "I can't wait to hear you act it out."

Anna closed her eyes and tried to feel like the girl in the play. When she opened her eyes, she looked at Lulu. Lulu is my mother, she thought, and she's broken a promise to me.

Anna read the girl's first speech.

GIRL: You told me I could have a pony when I was ten years old.

MOTHER: That's not what I said.

GIRL: You did, Mom. Honest. I have been waiting two whole years for a pony.

MOTHER: I said we would *think* about getting you a pony when you were ten. I thought about it. I have decided you *cannot* have a pony.

GIRL: We have a big yard. I'll take care of my pony. You won't have to do anything. Please, Mom. I love ponies so much.

MOTHER: Don't argue with me.

GIRL: But you said —

MOTHER: (*shouting*) The answer is final! No pony.

GIRL: (*crying softly*) But you promised.

THE END

When Anna acted the girl's last line, she felt tears welling up in her eyes.

Lulu stared at her. "You're really crying," she whispered.

Pam clapped. "Anna, that was wonderful," she said. "I told you that you were a great actor."

Anna looked down at the page she'd just read. It was fun to act from someone else's words.

"You have to try out for *Magic Pony*," said Lulu. "You and Acorn would have so much fun being in a play together."

Pam came over and sat on the rock next to Anna. "Acorn will get the part for sure," she said. "Remember how great he was in the movie."

Acorn had been in a feature movie, *Megan's Last Ride*, with a famous actor, Bette Fleming. In the movie, Acorn acted like he loved Bette, and Anna had been jealous. Anna had thought Acorn liked Bette more than her. What if Acorn gets a part in *Magic Pony* and I don't, wondered Anna. Will I be jealous again?

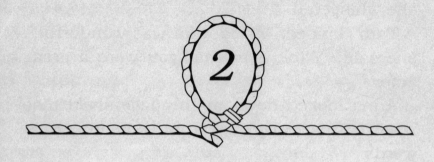

Tryouts

That night, Anna went out to the paddock to say good night to Acorn. She leaned against her pony's side and scratched his withers. Anna remembered being in the circus with Acorn. She had been a clown, and Acorn had pulled a cart. Anna loved entertaining the crowds with her pony. When I was a clown, I didn't have to memorize lines, thought Anna. What if I get the part in *Magic Pony* and I can't remember my lines?

Anna thought about how her mind worked. She was a good thinker and problem solver. She also loved to draw and paint. But Anna was dyslexic, so reading and writing were difficult for her. Memorizing words was difficult, too. When the Pony Pals studied together, Pam and Lulu remembered facts easily. Sometimes I can't remember, no matter how long I study, thought Anna. That's why Pam and Lulu always get better grades than me.

Pam Crandal was the best student in their class at Wiggins Elementary. Pam also knew the most about horses and ponies. Her mother was a riding teacher, and her father was a veterinarian. There were a lot of horses and ponies at the Crandals'. Pam had been riding for as long as she could remember.

Mrs. Crandal taught Anna how to ride, too. Learning how to ride was easy for me, thought Anna. I wish memorizing were just as easy.

Lulu Sanders had a terrific memory. She remembered all sorts of interesting facts, especially about animals. Lulu's father was a naturalist. Mr. Sanders traveled all over the world to study wild animals and their environments. Lulu's mother died when Lulu was little. After that, she traveled with her father. When Lulu turned ten, she moved to Wiggins to live with her grandmother. Now she was a Pony Pal.

Acting the lines Pam wrote was fun, thought Anna. I felt like I was the girl who wanted a pony. If I could remember the lines, I would love to be an actor.

Acorn nuzzled Anna's shoulder again and sighed.

Anna kissed his forehead. "Thanks," she said. "I love you, too."

The next morning, Lulu and Pam helped Anna groom Acorn for the tryouts. When the three girls rode their ponies across the town green, Acorn held his head up and pranced.

"I think Acorn knows something special is happening," said Lulu.

Anna felt nervous and scared. She wished she was confident like Acorn.

The three girls dismounted their ponies and led them to the small park behind the library. Some children and adults were already there. A red-haired man stood at a small table. He had a pile of papers in one hand and a megaphone in the other.

"That must be the director," Pam whispered to Anna.

Rosalie Lacey ran toward the Pony Pals. Rosalie was a six-year-old who adored ponies. "Acorn!" she shouted as she gave her favorite pony a big hug.

Anna looked around to see if Rosalie's brother, Mike, and his friend Tommy Rand were there. She didn't see Tommy, but Mike was following his sister, Rosalie. Anna remembered that Tommy was at sleep-away camp for a month. Mike and Tommy were two annoying older boys who liked to tease the Pony Pals.

Five-year-old Mimi Kline and her little Shetland pony, Tongo, joined the Pony Pals. "Tongo's going to be in the play," bragged Mimi.

"He's going to *try out* for the play," Rosalie corrected her.

"Are all your ponies going to try out?" Mimi asked Lulu.

"Just Acorn," answered Lulu.

Mimi took Anna's hand. "If Tongo wins, will you still be my friend?" she asked.

Anna laughed. "Of course I will," she answered.

"Rema Baxter is here," Lulu whispered to Anna. "Behind you."

None of the Pony Pals liked Rema Baxter. She owned Snow White before Lulu. Rema thought she was a big shot because she was older than the Pony Pals. She could also be a little mean. Anna thought that Rema Baxter and Tommy Rand had a lot in common. She wondered if Rema was trying out for the play.

Anna looked around for Rema. She was dressed in high-heeled sandals and standing near the director.

The director held the megaphone to his

mouth to speak. "Could I have your attention, please?" he said in a deep, strong voice.

Everyone stopped talking and turned toward him.

"I'm William Prentice, the writer and director of *Magic Pony*," he announced proudly.

A few people clapped.

"The Wiggins Players are taking the adult roles in the play," he continued. "Today's auditions are to cast the parts of a girl, Princess Kalandra; a boy, Joseph; and the Magic Pony. Let me tell you a little bit about the story."

Anna put her arm around Acorn's neck and waited for William to begin. She loved stories.

"*Magic Pony* takes place a long time ago in a faraway land," William began. "The main character is Princess Kalandra. The lovely Kalandra has a very serious illness that will kill her. Since early childhood, Kalandra has heard stories about a magical pony in the woods near the castle."

"Why is it a magic pony?" Rosalie shouted out.

"I was coming to that," answered William patiently. "One magical thing is that the pony has lived for *hundreds* of years."

"The pony must be a ghost," Mimi told Anna.

"The other magical thing about the pony," continued William, "is that it can heal terrible illnesses."

"The princess should look for that pony," Rosalie whispered to Anna.

"Kalandra dresses like an ordinary person," said William, "and goes into the woods. She climbs into a tree house. From there she looks for the Magic Pony. Kalandra doesn't see the pony, but she does spot a young woodsman. This is Joseph, and Kalandra is in his tree house. Joseph and Kalandra meet and become friends. Kalandra doesn't tell Joseph that she is sick or that she is the princess. But she does tell him that she is searching for the pony. Joseph offers to help Kalandra find the Magic Pony."

William stopped and looked around at his audience.

"Does the princess find the Magic Pony?" shouted Mimi.

"You'll learn the answer to that question when you come to the play," answered William. "But I will tell you one more thing: Joseph lives with his uncle Damien. Damien is an evil man who is also looking for the Magic Pony."

"I hope that bad uncle doesn't hurt the pony," Rosalie said to Anna.

William held up some sheets of paper. "Whoever is trying out for Princess Kalandra raise your hands."

Anna looked around. Three girls she recognized from the seventh grade and Rema Baxter put up their hands.

"Raise your hand, Anna," Pam whispered.

Lulu raised Anna's hand for her.

"Come over to the table and sign up, girls," William instructed. "And take a copy of the tryout scene. You have ten minutes to prepare it."

"Do we have to memorize it *now*?" blurted out Anna.

"No," answered William. "You can read the part for the audition and the first few rehearsals."

Anna took the two pages from William and went back to Lulu and Pam.

"And who is here for the role of Joseph?" asked William.

Anna looked around. Mike Lacey was the only ten- to twelve-year-old boy in Library Park. He didn't have his hand up.

William looked right at Mike. "What about you, sir?" he asked.

"I'm just here because my sister wanted to come," said Mike. "I don't want to be in the play."

"But you know how to read," said William.

" 'Course I do," answered Mike.

William held a paper toward Mike. "Just help us out here today."

Rosalie looked up at her brother. "Please do it, Mike," she pleaded. "Please."

Mike shrugged. "Okay," he told William.

"Yea!" shouted Rosalie.

"But I won't be in the play," Mike added.

"Mike wouldn't do this if Tommy Rand was here," Lulu whispered to Pam.

"Tommy thinks acting is for sissies," said Pam.

Mike took the pages from William and looked them over. Anna wondered if Mike was scared, too.

Anna read the tryout scene to herself three times. She hoped that she didn't have to go first.

William looked down at the sign-up sheet. "Okay," he said. "We'll start with Rema Baxter."

Rema grinned at everyone as she walked up front.

"She thinks she is such a big shot," mumbled Lulu.

Rema and Mike read the two pages of dialogue.

"Mike's a good actor," said Pam in amazement.

Anna thought that Rema was very good, too.

"Thank you, Rema," said William. He looked down at the sign-up sheet. "Next, Anna Harley."

Results!

As Anna walked to the director's table, she pretended she was Kalandra. I'm very sick, thought Anna. I am going to die. Maybe the Magic Pony can save my life.

"Imagine you are in a tree house," William told Anna. "Joseph has discovered you there. Begin."

Anna read Kalandra's first speech to Mike. To Anna, Mike wasn't Mike anymore. He was Joseph. She felt like she was Kalandra.

After Anna's audition, four more girls tried out for the role of Kalandra.

When the last one finished, Pam squeezed Anna's hand. "You were the best," she whispered.

"I think Rema was better than me," said Anna. "And she looks more like a princess."

"She *wasn't* better than you," said Pam.

"And she looks like a snob," added Lulu.

"Attention, everyone," said William. "It's time to audition the ponies."

"Tongo first," shouted Mimi. She tugged on Tongo's lead rope, but the stubborn little pony didn't budge.

"I'm sorry, Mimi," William said. "But your pony is too small for the role of Magic Pony."

"That's okay," Rosalie told Mimi. "*I* think Tongo is a magic pony."

Mimi put her arm around Tongo's neck. "Me, too," she agreed.

William walked over to the hitching post. "That just leaves these three ponies," he said. He rubbed the upside-down heart on Lightning's forehead. "What a pretty pony. But she's too big for the Magic Pony."

"She is not trying out, anyway," said Pam.

William put a hand on Snow White's head.

"This pony has the size and look I'm going for," he said.

"Snow White isn't trying out, either," explained Lulu. "We just rode here."

Anna put a hand on Acorn's back. "Acorn's trying out," she explained.

"Acorn was in a Bette Fleming movie," said Lulu.

"And the Yellow Tent Circus," added Pam. "He knows lots of tricks."

"Very impressive," said William.

Rema came up beside William. "Snow White used to be *my* pony," she bragged. She smiled at William.

Anna stepped forward. "Snow White is Lulu's pony now," she told William.

"Do you four girls work with one another's ponies?" he asked.

"Yes," said the Pony Pals in unison.

"Snow White would do anything I tell her," added Rema.

Anna and Lulu exchanged a glance. Rema Baxter didn't even *like* ponies anymore.

William pointed to Snow White and Acorn.

24

"I'd like to see both of these ponies follow-ing commands," he said.

"Let Snow White try out," Anna whispered to Lulu. "It'll be fun."

"Okay," agreed Lulu. "But Acorn will get the part. Snow White doesn't know even one trick."

William had Snow White and Acorn walk up and down and stop on command. He didn't ask the ponies to do any tricks.

Next, William asked the girls who tried out if they could ride bareback. Anna, Rema, and one other girl said they could.

After the ponies auditioned, William thanked everyone for coming. "I'll post the results of the tryouts tomorrow morning at nine," he said. "The list will be on the library bulletin board. I'll give out scripts in the library."

As the Pony Pals were leaving, Rema came up to them. "You were very good, Anna," she said. "You'll make a good actress when you grow up." She kissed Snow White's cheek. "Bye for now, my magic pony."

Rema smiled her fake smile at the Pony Pals and left.

"She didn't like Snow White that much when she owned her," said Pam.

"She thinks she's going to be Kalandra," said Lulu. "She's so conceited."

"Well, Acorn's going to be the Magic Pony, anyway," said Lulu. "Acorn's the best pony actor." She put an arm around Anna's shoulder. "And you'll be Kalandra. You were the best girl actor."

"Mike was the best boy actor," said Rosalie proudly.

"He was the *only* boy actor," Pam reminded her with a giggle. "But you're right. He *was* good."

Anna noticed that William was talking to Mike. She wondered if Mike Lacey would agree to be in the play after all.

The next morning, the Pony Pals gathered around the library bulletin board. The first thing Anna noticed was her own name.

"Anna, you're Kalandra!" exclaimed Pam.

"But Acorn is just an understudy," said Lulu with surprise.

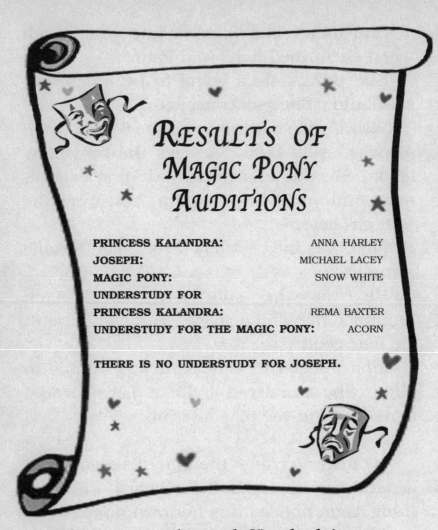

RESULTS OF MAGIC PONY AUDITIONS

PRINCESS KALANDRA:	ANNA HARLEY
JOSEPH:	MICHAEL LACEY
MAGIC PONY:	SNOW WHITE
UNDERSTUDY FOR PRINCESS KALANDRA:	REMA BAXTER
UNDERSTUDY FOR THE MAGIC PONY:	ACORN

THERE IS NO UNDERSTUDY FOR JOSEPH.

"What's an understudy?" asked Anna.

"It's the person who takes your place if you get sick," explained Pam.

"Acorn should be the Magic Pony," said Lulu. "Not Snow White."

"That's okay," said Anna. "Snow White will make a great Magic Pony."

Anna didn't tell her friends that she was really disappointed that Acorn wasn't in the play with her. I only tried out because of Acorn, she thought.

Mike came out of the library. He carried a script for *Magic Pony*.

"Mike, you were really good yesterday," said Pam.

"So?" said Mike. "It's no big deal. It's just something to do."

Something to do while Tommy Rand is at camp, thought Anna. Tommy will be at camp until the play is over. Anna knew Mike wouldn't be in the play if Tommy were around.

"Come on, Anna," said Pam. "You have to pick up your script, too."

The three friends headed into the library.

"Can we read it with you?" asked Lulu.

"Of course," answered Anna as she pushed opened the library door.

"I can't wait to find out what happens to Kalandra and Joseph," said Pam.

William was at the front desk, talking to the librarian. "Here's our Kalandra," he announced happily. He held out a script. "For you. I've highlighted all of your lines in pink."

"Thank you," said Anna.

William turned to Lulu. "Snow White is the perfect Magic Pony," he exclaimed. "Absolutely perfect."

"I think that Acorn is a better actor," said Lulu.

"Maybe you're right," said William. "But Snow White *looks* the part. We'll put some silver sparkles on that beautiful white coat. She'll glow in the dark woods behind the library. It will all be very magical."

William gave Anna a rehearsal schedule, too. "I won't need Snow White for a few days," he told Lulu. "Anna will let you know when."

As the Pony Pals left, Anna flipped through the script. Many of the speeches were highlighted in pink. How could she ever memorize all her lines in two weeks?

30

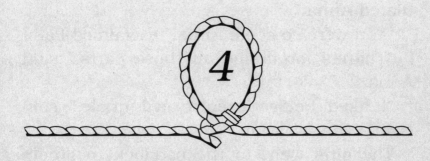

Blood for Gold

"Let's go back to Anna's and read the play," said Lulu. "I want to know what happens to Kalandra and Joseph."

"We can read it out loud and take parts," suggested Pam. "That way you can start practicing right away, Anna."

"Great idea," agreed Lulu. She grinned at Anna. "Okay with you, Princess Kalandra?"

"Yes, my loyal subjects," teased Anna.

A few minutes later, the three friends sat at the Harleys' picnic table. When they had

read the whole play, Lulu and Pam congrat-
ulated Anna.

"You were so good, Anna!" exclaimed Pam.

"Thanks for taking all those parts," said
Anna.

"I liked being Joseph's evil uncle," said
Lulu. "That was fun."

The girls went to the paddock to groom
their ponies. While they worked, they talked
about the play.

"I hate how Joseph's uncle Damien wants
to kill the Magic Pony for her blood," said
Anna.

"*We will sell that pony's blood for gold,
Joseph!*" said Lulu, repeating a line from the
play.

"Damien believes only an innocent girl can
catch the pony," said Pam as she ran the
brush along Lightning's side. "That's why he
lets Joseph play with Kalandra. He wants
Kalandra to lead him to the pony."

Anna used the currycomb on Acorn's side.
"Joseph and Kalandra are both keeping
secrets," she said.

"Joseph doesn't tell Kalandra that his uncle wants the pony," said Lulu.

"Kalandra has two secrets from Joseph," added Pam. "One is that she is sick, and the other is that she is a princess."

"I like that Kalandra and Joseph still become great friends," said Lulu as she wiped down Snow White's neck. "And they look for the Magic Pony together. They make a great team."

That night, Anna sat on her bed and read the play again. She loved the story of the *Magic Pony*. She especially liked the scene when Kalandra and the Magic Pony finally meet. Kalandra is sitting in a field by herself, waiting for Joseph. While she waits, she sings a lullaby about a magic pony. Suddenly, the Magic Pony comes out of the woods and walks over to her. She tells the pony that she is dying, and that riding the pony could save her life. Joseph overhears this. Now he knows that his friend is sick. He is about to warn Kalandra about his uncle, when Damien appears.

Joseph tells Kalandra to escape on the Magic Pony. Kalandra jumps on the pony and rides off.

Anna yawned. She was too tired to reread the last scene.

The next morning, the Pony Pals left their ponies in the Harley paddock and walked to the library.

"You don't have to stay for the whole rehearsal," Anna told her friends. "It might be boring." She looked at the blue sky. "It's a great day for a trail ride."

"Maybe we'll go riding after lunch," agreed Pam.

"What about Acorn?" asked Lulu. "Can Rosalie ride him?"

"Sure," agreed Anna.

Mike and Rema were already at the park behind the library. William was talking to a man and woman. They must be the actors playing Damien and the Queen, thought Anna.

When Rema saw Anna, she stood up.

"Sorry," she said with a smile. "This is your seat."

Anna smiled back. She was surprised that Rema was being friendly.

William introduced the other actors to Anna, Mike, and Rema. "By the way," he said, "we're building a tree house for the play." William pointed to a tall oak tree. "The tree house will be in that tree," he continued. "It will be ready for tomorrow's rehearsal." He looked around at his cast. "Now we'll have a read-through of the play, starting with line one, page one."

Anna loved acting out the play with the other actors.

When they finished reading, William looked around at his actors. "Very good, everyone," he said.

"Adults, that's it for you today," continued William. "Mike, Rema, and Anna, I'll see you back here at one o'clock sharp."

Rema and Rosalie walked over to Anna and Mike.

"Pam and Lulu went back to your house," Rosalie told Anna. "They said to meet them there."

Rema smiled at Anna. "You were great," she said.

"Thanks," said Anna.

"Mike was great, too!" Rosalie said proudly.

"They were both great," concluded Rema.

Anna ran over to Lulu's house. Pam and Anna were putting food on the picnic table.

While they ate, Pam asked Anna about the rehearsal.

"Rema is being nice to me," said Anna. "Really friendly."

"Don't trust her, Anna," said Lulu. "She can be a real phony."

"Sometimes people change," said Anna.

"Not Rema," said Lulu. Pam nodded in agreement.

Rosalie Lacey ran into the yard. She shouted hi to the Pony Pals and went right to the paddock. "We're going on a trail ride, Acorn," she called out. Acorn ran up to the fence to meet her.

Lulu looked at her watch. "It's one-ten, Anna," she said. "What time is your rehearsal?"

Anna grabbed her script and jumped up from the bench. "I'm late," she said.

As Anna ran across the town green, she thought, I didn't even say good-bye to Acorn. She wished that she could be at rehearsal *and* go for a trail ride on her pony.

When Anna reached Library Park, Mike and Rema were rehearsing the first scene. Anna noticed that they weren't looking at the script. They'd already memorized the scene.

Rema saw Anna and smiled. "Where are your friends?" she asked.

"They went on a trail ride," answered Anna.

"My sister went, too," added Mike.

"Don't you miss riding, Anna?" asked Rema. "I thought you loved riding more than anything."

"I do," agreed Anna. She looked at her script. "But I like acting, too."

Rema put an arm around Anna's shoulder. "You look like a princess," she said. "You make the perfect Kalandra."

"Let's go," shouted William. "Mike and Anna, we'll try that first scene without the scripts. You can hold them and look when you need to. That okay with you, Mike?"

"Sure," said Mike. "I already know it."

"And you, Anna?"

Anna felt a lump rise up in her throat. She nodded.

"Go ahead then, Anna," said William. "You have the first line."

At least I know the first line, thought Anna. She pretended she was Kalandra in the tree house, looking in the woods. *"Magic Pony, where did you go?"* she said.

"Anna," corrected William, "the line is *Magic Pony, where are you?"*

Anna looked down at her script. William was right.

I couldn't even remember the first line, thought Anna. How am I going to memorize a whole play?

Riding Bareback

Anna felt embarrassed through the whole rehearsal. Mike knew a lot of his lines by heart. But Anna couldn't remember any of hers. She was glad when the rehearsal was over.

"No rehearsals tomorrow," William announced. "Use the day to memorize your parts. The next rehearsal is Wednesday at ten A.M. See you then."

Anna closed her script and started to leave. Rema ran to catch up with her. "Anna, do you know how actors remember their lines?" she asked.

"No," answered Anna. "How?"

"It's very easy," she said. "Just read your part a few times, and you'll remember it. That's what professional actors do."

"Thanks for the tip," said Anna. She felt better as she walked around to the front of the library. Remembering lines in a play was different from remembering schoolwork.

"It's great to see you and Lulu and Pam again," said Rema. "I want you all to come for a sleepover at my house tomorrow night. You and your ponies. They can stay in Snow White's old paddock."

Anna couldn't believe her ears. Rema was inviting them to a party!

"It'll be a lot of fun," continued Rema. "We can play with your ponies, watch videos, and have pizza."

Will Pam and Lulu want to go to Rema's for a sleepover? wondered Anna.

A horn honked. It was Rema's father, waiting to give her a ride home.

"Gotta go," said Rema. "Come to my house at four tomorrow. I'll be waiting for you."

Rema was gone before Anna could say, *I have to ask Lulu and Pam about the sleepover.*

Anna walked back to her yard. She hoped her friends were back from the trail ride. But they hadn't returned. Anna felt lonesome without her friends and her pony. She leaned against the apple tree and opened her script. Before she'd finished page two, her eyes closed and she fell asleep.

Anna woke to the sound of laughter and pounding hooves. She walked over to the paddock to meet her friends and her pony.

"We had so much fun!" exclaimed Rosalie as she jumped off Acorn. "Acorn's the best. Can I take off his saddle and cool him down?"

"Okay," agreed Anna.

"It was a good ride," Lulu told Anna. "We saw a fox and three deer."

"And some bunnies," added Rosalie. "They were so cute."

"I don't have rehearsal tomorrow," Anna told them. "I can go for a trail ride with you."

"Great," said Lulu.

"And guess what?" added Anna. "Rema invited us to a sleepover."

"Rema?!" exclaimed Lulu. "Why?"

"She likes us," answered Anna. "I told you she's been really nice to me."

"I don't want to go to Rema's," said Lulu.

"I do," said Anna, putting her hands on her hips. "I think we should give Rema a second chance."

"Maybe Rema's changed," agreed Pam.

"I think she's the same snobby Rema," said Lulu. "But we can go to her dumb old party. You'll see that I'm right."

The next morning, Anna read through the script two times. She didn't tell her friends Rema's advice: *Just read your part a few times, and you'll remember it. That's what professional actors do.*

In the afternoon, the Pony Pals went for a picnic and trail ride. At three-thirty, they put their sleeping bags on the back of their saddles and rode over to Rema's.

Rema was waiting for them in the paddock. She waved and shouted, "Hello!" The Pony Pals waved back. Anna hoped that they would have a good time at Rema's.

Rema helped them unsaddle their ponies and cool them down. She ran a hand along Snow White's neck. "You are such a good pony," she said.

Snow White nuzzled Rema.

Rema smiled at Lulu. "She remembers me," she said. "Can I ride her bareback? I used to love to do that."

"Aren't you too big to ride Snow White?" asked Lulu.

"Let me try," said Rema. "For old times' sake."

Pam helped Rema mount. At first, Rema slipped around on Snow White's back.

Snow White was patient with his old rider. After a few tries, Rema rode with better balance.

Anna and Lulu exchanged a glance. Anna

knew that Lulu didn't like Rema riding Snow White.

When Rema dismounted, she handed the reins back to Lulu. "I'm so glad you have Snow White," she said. "Thanks for letting me ride her."

"You're welcome," mumbled Lulu.

"I rented a terrific video," announced Rema. "It's an adventure movie about Connemara ponies in Ireland." She smiled at Pam. "I thought you'd like it because Lightning is a Connemara pony."

"Lightning was born in Ireland," said Pam. "I can't wait to see the movie."

The four girls sat around in Rema's room and watched the video. Anna thought it was the best movie about ponies she'd ever seen. Lulu and Pam liked it, too.

Rema hit the rewind button on the VCR. "Let's make pizza now," she suggested. "I have all these great toppings."

The girls went downstairs to the kitchen. By the time they finished making and eating pizza, it was dark out.

"Next, let's play cards," suggested Rema. She smiled at Anna. "You can choose the game."

"Do you know how to play Hearts?" Anna asked. "That's my favorite card game."

"Hearts is my favorite card game, too!" exclaimed Rema. She smiled at Pam. "Whenever I play it, I remember Lightning's upside-down heart."

The Pony Pals and Rema stayed up late playing cards and talking. Rema told them funny stories about being at boarding school. Pam and Anna told her some of their Pony Pal adventures.

At ten o'clock, Pam stretched her arms and yawned. "I'm tired," she announced.

"Me, too," agreed Lulu. She knelt to unroll her sleeping bag.

"Guess what?" said Rema. "I got us *three* kinds of ice cream and we have sugar cones. Let's go make ice-cream cones."

"Yum," said Anna as she rolled off her sleeping bag.

"Sounds great," agreed Pam.

It was past midnight when the Pony Pals and Rema finally went to bed.

Anna lay in her sleeping bag and thought about the fun party.

Little snoring sounds came from Rema's bed.

Anna looked over at Lulu in her sleeping bag. She was awake.

"I told you Rema's changed," Anna whispered.

Lulu sat up on her elbow to face Anna. "I still don't trust her," she said.

"Why not?" asked Anna. "She planned a great party for us."

"She invited us because she wanted to ride Snow White," answered Lulu in a hushed voice. "If you get sick and can't be in the play, Rema would have your part. She'd be Kalandra and have to ride Snow White bareback."

"But the videos and pizza and ice cream," protested Anna. "She's been so nice to us."

"I'll never trust Rema Baxter and neither should you," scolded Lulu. She lay back down and closed her eyes.

Anna rolled over and closed her eyes, too. Rema's helping me, she thought. She told me how to remember my speeches for the play. Anna wished Lulu would change her mind about Rema.

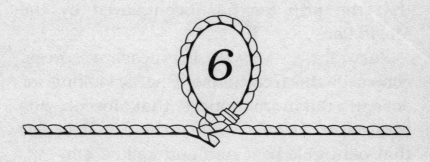

In the Tree House

The tree house was ready for rehearsal the next day. Mike, Anna, and William climbed up the ladder. One side of the tree house had a low railing instead of a wall. "That's so the audience can have a good view of you," William explained.

Mike and Anna acted out three tree-house scenes for William. Mike knew all his lines, even the ones for the last scene of the play.

The scene opens with Joseph alone in the tree house. He hasn't seen Kalandra since she escaped on the Magic Pony.

Joseph learns from a passing huntsman that the princess has been saved by the Magic Pony.

Kalandra, dressed in peasant dress, comes to the tree house. She is looking for Joseph. Kalandra notices that Joseph has bruises on his face and arm. He tells her that his uncle beat him and kicked him out. *"Why?"* asks Kalandra.

"Because I let you escape on the Magic Pony," admits Joseph.

Joseph asks Kalandra if she is the princess. She admits that she is. Kalandra invites Joseph to live in the castle. He can be a groomsman and take care of the ponies. *"Will I be taking care of the Magic Pony?"* Joseph asks.

Kalandra says that the pony is free. She rode her to a different forest. *"So she'll be safe from your uncle,"* she adds.

"Can we go to that forest someday and look for the Magic Pony?" asks Joseph.

Kalandra smiles at her new friend and says, *"Yes."*

Anna-as-Kalandra smiled at Mike-as-Joseph and said, *"Yes."*

The scene was over.

Anna loved acting the scene. But she hated that she didn't know her lines by heart. She also felt very, very tired.

William patted Mike on the back. "Good work," he said. "Now I want to speak to Anna privately. We'll meet you down below."

Mike went down the ladder, and Anna stayed in the tree house with William.

"Anna, what time did you go to bed last night?" he asked.

"Pretty late," Anna admitted.

"You certainly didn't stay up studying your part," he continued. "Did you study it at all?"

"I did," answered Anna.

"Well, you obviously didn't study enough," he scolded. "You needed to look at your script for *every* line. Rema knows all Kalandra's lines, and she's just the understudy."

"I'm sorry," said Anna. Her throat tightened with tears.

"Here comes Snow White," Rema called up to them.

William climbed down the ladder. As Anna followed, tears sprung to her eyes.

"Anna, we'll rehearse the scene where the Magic Pony comes to you," William called up to her.

Anna swallowed her tears. She didn't want anyone to see that she was upset.

"Lulu, bring Snow White to the woods on my right," instructed William. "Anna, you come out of the woods on my left. Sit in the field and sing the lullaby. Then signal Snow White to come to you."

Anna went to the edge of the woods. I'm not a good actor, she thought. I can't remember my lines, and my voice isn't loud enough. Anna wanted to run away. If Acorn were here, I'd ride off on him, she thought.

"Anna, let's go!" shouted William. "The scene starts on page forty-four."

Anna turned to page forty-four and walked out of the woods. She sat on a big rock and sang the lullaby.

"We can barely hear you, Anna," barked William. "Start over."

Anna started over, but her voice was shaking.

Snow White walked out of the woods, and Anna cracked a carrot behind her back.

Snow White looked at Anna, then turned and walked over to Rema's side. The white pony lowered her head toward Rema.

"Why did the pony go to Rema?" asked William.

"Snow White was *my* pony," answered Rema. "We have a special connection." She hugged Snow White. "My beautiful pony."

"Anna, I thought you were going to teach Snow White that trick," said William.

"She didn't learn it yet," said Anna.

"Well, she did it for Rema," William pointed out. He looked at his watch. "That's enough for today. The next rehearsal is at ten A.M. tomorrow. And Anna, please learn your lines, and *please* work with Snow White."

The Pony Pals took Snow White back to the paddock.

"I hate that Snow White went right to Rema," complained Lulu. "Anna, you need to rehearse with Snow White."

"I know," mumbled Anna. She didn't feel like talking to her friends.

When they reached the paddock, Anna went into the shed for Acorn's saddle.

"What are you doing?" asked Pam.

"I'm going for a trail ride," answered Anna. "Alone."

"I thought you had to study your lines," said Pam.

"And work with Snow White," added Lulu.

Anna put the saddle on Acorn's back. "I'll do it later," she said.

"We already went for a trail ride today," said Lulu, "with Rosalie."

"I know," said Anna as she slipped on Acorn's bridle. "I told you I want to go alone."

Lulu and Pam exchanged a glance. Anna didn't care what they thought she should or should not do.

She pulled down the stirrups and tightened the girth.

"Why are you running off by yourself?" asked Lulu. "Is it because of the play?"

"I already told you," answered Anna. "I just want to go for a ride."

Anna jumped on Acorn and rode onto Pony Pal Trail.

"Anna, stop!" Pam shouted after her.

"We should talk about what's bothering you," added Lulu.

As Anna rode along the trail, she thought about the play. Rema had already memorized a lot of Kalandra's lines. Snow White went to Rema instead of her. They were perfect together.

"I didn't want to be in the play without you, anyway," Anna told her pony. She moved him into a canter.

When they turned onto the Wiggins trails, Anna slowed Acorn down. Then she urged Acorn to canter again. Acorn didn't go any faster. Anna noticed a shine of sweat along his neck.

"I'm sorry I worked you so hard," she said.

She patted Acorn's hot neck. "You can cool off at the brook."

Anna sat by the side of Badd Brook and watched her pony drink. She tried skipping a stone. It sank. I'm going to call William as soon as I get home, she thought. I'll tell him I can't be in the play.

Anna heard a whinny in the distance.

Acorn looked up and whinnied back.

"Shh," Anna scolded. "They'll find us."

A minute later, Pam and Lulu rode into the clearing beside the brook.

Anna stood up. "Why are you following me?" she asked angrily.

"We weren't *following* you," said Pam. "We were *looking* for you."

"We want to have a barn sleepover tonight," added Lulu. "We have a Pony Pal Problem and we need three ideas."

"Do you think that *I'm* a Pony Pal Problem?" asked Anna.

"The play is the problem," answered Lulu. "And it's making problems for you."

"Please have a meeting with us about it," begged Pam.

Anna looked from Pam to Lulu. Pam looked worried, and Lulu looked sad.

"Okay," agreed Anna. "We can have a sleepover."

"And a meeting with three ideas?" asked Pam.

Anna nodded.

I already have my idea, she thought. And it's the only idea we need to solve this Pony Pal Problem.

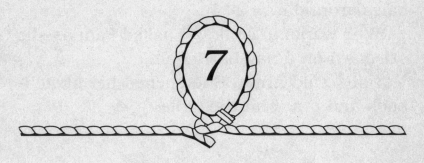

Three Ideas

The Pony Pals rode back to Pam's and went to the Crandals' kitchen. While they had cookies and milk, they each thought of an idea and wrote it down. Anna drew her idea.

Pam took a last bite of cookie and closed her notebook. "Let's share ideas in the hayloft instead of here," she suggested.

"Okay," agreed Anna as she added a final line to her drawing.

A few minutes later, the Pony Pals climbed the ladder to the hayloft.

Pam pulled out two big hay bales to use

for a table. Lulu and Anna put three hay bales around it.

"Who wants to go first?" asked Pam as she sat down on a hay-bale chair.

"I do," said Anna. She opened her sketch-book and put it on the table.

"My idea is that Rema should be Kalandra instead of me," explained Anna. "I'm a Pony Pal, not an actor."

"You can be a Pony Pal *and* an actor," protested Pam.

"Besides, you can't let Rema be in a play with Snow White," said Lulu. "She acts like Snow White is still her pony. I hate that."

"But I don't want to be in the play," said Anna.

"Why?" asked Pam.

Anna looked at her hands. "I can't remember my lines," she mumbled. "I'm dumb."

"You are *not* dumb, Anna Harley," said Lulu. "It just takes a long time for you to memorize things."

"That's what my idea is about," said Pam. She handed her idea to Anna to read out loud.

Lulu and I should help Anna learn her lines.

"We'll rehearse with you until you learn your lines," said Pam. "We'll help you study."

"Just like we do with homework," added Lulu.

"Rema already told me how actors study their lines," said Anna.

"What did she tell you?" asked Lulu suspiciously.

"Actors remember their lines by reading the script a few times," said Anna. "It's different than memorizing in school." Anna nervously twisted a piece of straw around

her finger. "But it didn't work for me."

"It didn't work because it's a stupid idea," said Pam.

Lulu stood up. "Rema was trying to trick you," she said angrily. "She doesn't want you to learn the part. *She* wants to be Kalandra. That's why she's been so friendly to us and to Snow White."

"But even Snow White knows that Rema should be Kalandra," said Anna. "She went to Rema instead of me. Remember?"

"I think Rema had a piece of peppermint in her lap," said Pam. "Snow White heard the plastic wrapper rattle and went to Rema for a treat."

Lulu spun around. "That's it!" she exclaimed. "Snow White loves peppermints, and Rema always gave them to her."

"And I think Rema had that sleepover to keep Anna busy," said Pam. "She didn't want you to study your lines, Anna."

Lulu turned to Anna. "I told you not to trust her," she said.

"Even if you're right about Rema," said

Anna, "I still don't want to be in the play. I miss Acorn."

"That's what my idea is about," said Lulu, opening her notebook.

She read her idea to her friends.

Acorn should be in the play instead of Snow White.

"Snow White only got the part because she's white," said Lulu. "She doesn't know any tricks or how to act. Acorn is a real star pony. He should be the Magic Pony, not the understudy."

"We could put gold sparkles on his coat," suggested Pam. "That would make him look very magical."

"Let's bring Acorn to William and tell him our idea," said Lulu. "We'll show him how great Acorn is."

"It would be so wonderful if you and Acorn were in a play together, Anna," added Pam.

Anna tied a piece of hay into a knot. "But I don't know my lines," she said sadly.

"We'll help you," said Pam. "You can learn them. I know you can do it."

"Anna, you should memorize your scene with Acorn first," suggested Lulu. "You and Acorn can act it out for William."

Pam stood up. "Let's work on that scene right now," she said.

"I left my script in the paddock," confessed Anna. "We have to go back to my house."

Pam reached into her backpack and pulled out the script. "I brought it," she said.

Anna smiled and took the script from her. "I'll try your ideas," she said, "but if they don't work, I'm dropping out. Okay?"

"Okay," said Pam. "But you have to try really hard."

"I will," agreed Anna.

First, Anna memorized the lines for the lullaby. Next, she studied the lines for when Joseph finds her with the pony. Lulu took the part of Mike. In an hour, Anna had memorized her lines for the whole scene.

"Now, let's go practice with Acorn," suggested Pam.

The three friends went down the ladder and out to the paddock.

Anna sat on a big rock in the field. Lulu led Acorn to the edge of the field.

When Anna sang the lullaby, Acorn looked at her. She gave her pony the signal to come to her. Acorn came over. As Anna continued singing, she gave Acorn the signal to bow. He did.

"*Magic Pony,*" said Anna-as-Kalandra. "*I am very sick and will die soon. I am too young to die. Will you save my life?*"

Acorn raised his head and nodded once.

"That was so beautiful," said Lulu.

"You remembered your lines perfectly," added Pam, looking up from the script. "You didn't make one mistake."

Anna brushed Acorn's mane off his forehead. "Good work, Acorn," she said.

"I hope William will let Acorn be in the play instead of Snow White," said Lulu.

Me, too, thought Anna. Me, too. And I hope I can remember my lines.

Back in Town

The next morning, Anna and Lulu rode home on Pony Pal Trail. Anna repeated her lines to herself the whole way.

By the time they reached the paddock, the rehearsal was about to begin.

"I'll take Acorn's tack off," Lulu told Anna.

Anna grabbed her script out of the saddle-bag. "Thanks," she told Lulu.

Anna was running across the town green when a boy on a bike barreled toward her. As the bike screeched to a halt, it bumped into her.

Anna fell on her behind.

Tommy Rand was looking down on her. "Hey, Pony Pest," he said. "What are you doing on the ground?"

"You jerk, Tommy!" Anna shouted. "You could have killed me."

Anna stood up and brushed off her backside. "I thought you were at camp," she said. "Did you get kicked out?"

"Who cares?" Tommy sneered. "You seen Mike?"

Anna knew that Mike was probably at the play rehearsal behind Library Park. But she didn't want Tommy to know that. If he teases Mike about being in a play, thought Anna, Mike will drop out. The play couldn't go on without a Joseph.

"Maybe Mike took Rosalie to the lake," suggested Anna. "He's been baby-sitting for her."

Tommy turned his bike around and peeled off toward the lake. He didn't say good-bye or thank-you. Typical Tommy, thought Anna.

70

When Anna got to rehearsal, Mike was under the tree house talking to Rema.

"Hi, Anna," Rema said cheerfully.

Anna didn't feel very cheerful about seeing Rema. But she said hi, anyway.

"Kalandra and Joseph, come on up," William called from the tree house.

Anna followed Mike up the ladder. "Tommy was looking for you," she told him.

Mike turned from the top rung. "What'd you tell him?" he asked in a nervous voice.

"That you were probably at the lake with Rosalie," answered Anna.

"Thanks," mumbled Mike.

Anna's heart pounded as they began rehearsal. What if, after all her work, she couldn't remember her lines? But she didn't forget them. She didn't have to look at her script once during the first scene. Mike had to look at his script a lot.

At the end of the rehearsal, William smiled at Anna. "Well done, Anna," he said. He turned to Mike. "You knew all your lines yesterday, Mike. What happened?"

"Nothing," answered Mike.

I know what happened, thought Anna. He's afraid Tommy will show up here.

Mike and Anna rehearsed another tree-house scene.

Mike fumbled a lot of his lines. William told him to concentrate.

During the last scene, Mike was more distracted than ever. He kept looking out of the tree house instead of at Anna. He's looking for Tommy, thought Anna.

They did the scene three times. Mike didn't get any better.

"Let's take an hour break," William finally announced. "After lunch, we'll work with the pony."

Mike scampered down the ladder and across the yard. "Look over your part during lunch," William called after him.

Anna followed William down the ladder. Pam and Lulu met her.

"I didn't know you were here," Anna said with surprise.

Pam grinned and gave her an okay sign. "You were great," she said.

"Terrific," agreed Lulu. "But Mike wasn't so good. I thought you said he knew his lines."

"Tommy Rand is back in town," Anna told them.

"Uh-oh," said Lulu. "That's not so good for Mike."

"Do you think Mike will drop out of the play?" whispered Pam.

Rema came up to the Pony Pals.

"I had so much fun with you guys the other night," she said, smiling at each of them. "Let's do it again. Come over to my house after rehearsal. I have some great new videos. We can make popcorn."

Anna and Lulu exchanged a glance. They were thinking the same thing. Rema was trying to keep Anna from studying her part.

"We can't go to your house today," said Pam.

"I have to study the script," added Anna.

Rema pouted. "You know your part perfectly," she said. "You don't have to study it anymore."

"Yes, I do," insisted Anna.

"Rema, you're just trying to distract Anna," said Lulu. "You want her part in the play."

Rema sneered at them. "You guys are making such a big deal out of this stupid kids' play." She threw down her script. "I'm fed up with the whole thing."

"She's just like Tommy Rand," Lulu said to Anna.

Rema went over to William and quit. He tried to convince her to stay and help out with the play. "You can be in charge of passing out programs," he offered.

"Forget it," said Rema. "I'm out of here."

"She's so rude," Pam whispered.

"Bye-bye, Pony Pests," said Rema as she walked away.

"Well, Anna," said William. "You'd better learn all your lines, and you'd better not get sick."

"I won't," said Anna. "I mean, I *won't* get sick and I *will* learn my lines."

"See you with the pony after lunch," he said.

Anna didn't tell William that she was bringing Acorn to the rehearsal instead of Snow White.

The girls went back to Anna's for lunch.

"I wonder if Mike will drop out of the play, too?" said Lulu.

Anna wondered the same thing. If Mike wasn't in the play, who would play Joseph?

Emergency Meeting

The girls had a quick lunch in Anna's kitchen. While Lulu cleaned up, Pam and Anna went out to the paddock. They groomed Acorn and Anna rehearsed with him one more time.

As the Pony Pals and Acorn walked across the town green, Rosalie ran up to them. She looked upset.

"How come you're alone, Rosalie?" asked Anna.

"Where's Mike?" asked Pam.

"He said to meet him here," answered Rosalie. "He was supposed to make me lunch." Tears came into her eyes. "What if Mike got hurt?"

"I bet he was hanging out with Tommy and forgot," said Lulu.

"I'm sure he's okay," added Anna.

"You can stay with us," suggested Pam. "You can watch the rehearsal."

Lulu patted Rosalie on the shoulder. "I'll go back to my house and get you a sandwich. Okay?"

Rosalie nodded and took Anna's hand.

Will Mike cut the rehearsal? Anna wondered.

The three girls and Acorn walked behind the library. William and the actor playing Damien were the only ones there.

William looked surprised to see Acorn. "Where's the white pony?" he asked.

"Can we rehearse with Acorn today?" asked Anna. "Acorn is Snow White's understudy."

"Snow White doesn't even know her part yet," said William. He was annoyed.

"Do you want us to go back and get Snow White?" asked Anna.

"Never mind," said William. "We can use the Shetland. But just for today's rehearsal." He looked around. "Now where's Mike?"

"He's hanging out with Tom — " began Rosalie.

Anna and Pam exchanged a quick glance. They didn't want Mike to get in trouble.

"Mike's not in the first part of the scene," said Pam, interrupting Rosalie. "You could rehearse that part."

William sighed. "All right," he agreed. "We might as well get started."

Pam led Acorn to the other side of Library Park, and Anna went to her spot in the woods.

While Anna waited, she saw Mike ride his bike into Library Park. Tommy wasn't with him. Did Mike tell Tommy about the play? Anna wondered.

When Anna walked out of the woods, she was Kalandra. As Kalandra, she sat on the rock and sang the lullaby.

Acorn came to her and bowed.

She told the Magic Pony that she was dying. *"Will you save me?"* she asked.

Acorn nodded.

Mike-as-Joseph came out of the woods and saw Kalandra with the Magic Pony. He tried to warn Kalandra about Damien. But it was too late. Damien found them and tried to capture the Magic Pony.

Anna-as-Kalandra jumped on the Magic Pony's back, rode across Library Park and into the woods.

After riding a short way, Anna turned Acorn around and rode him back into the park.

"Fabulous!" shouted the actor playing Damien.

Pam, Lulu, and Rosalie clapped.

"How'd you teach Acorn to do all that?" asked Mike.

Anna jumped off Acorn. She felt very proud of her pony. She felt proud of herself, too. She had remembered all her lines.

Rosalie ran over and hugged Acorn. He took a bite out of her sandwich.

Everyone laughed.

"Acorn knows lots of tricks," giggled Anna.

"Can the white pony do all of those tricks?" William asked Lulu.

"She knows the eating-the-sandwich trick," answered Lulu. "But that's all. Acorn is the actor."

"He was really good," said William.

Anna gave Acorn a signal and he bowed.

Everyone laughed again.

"We can put gold glitter on Acorn's coat," said Pam. "He'll look very magical."

"I'm announcing an official casting change," said William. "Acorn is the Magic Pony."

The Pony Pals shouted, "All right!" and hit high fives.

"Hey, what's going on here?" shouted a boy's voice.

Tommy Rand was speeding toward them on his bike. He screeched to a halt beside Mike.

"I was looking for you, man," he said. "You disappeared on me." He looked at each of the

Pony Pals. "What are you doing with the Pony Pests?"

"I have to watch Rosalie," said Mike.

"Mike's in the play," exclaimed Rosalie. "He's the star!"

Mike put out his hand to cover his sister's mouth. She wiggled away from him.

"Anna's a star and so is Acorn," continued Rosalie.

Tommy laughed out loud. Not a friendly laugh, but a mean one.

"And who are you?" William asked Tommy.

"What's it to you?" Tommy asked back.

William looked him up and down. "You are one tough guy," he said with a grin.

"His name's *Tommy*," said Rosalie. "He went to sleep-away camp."

"You seem pretty fast on that bike, Tommy," said William. "Can you ride it one-handed?"

" 'Course," answered Tommy. "I can ride no hands."

"Okay, everyone," said William. "Take a

five-minute break. I have to go inside for a minute."

William and the adult actor went into the library.

"Hey, Mike," said Tommy. "Let's get out of here."

"He can't leave," said Rosalie, "because he's in the play. They're practicing. The play's on Saturday. Are you going to come?"

"You're in a kiddie play!" Tommy shouted at Mike. "You're a sissy like those wimpy guys at that dumb camp."

"It's just a play," mumbled Mike.

Tommy laughed his mean laugh again. "How can you be in a play with the Pony Pests?" he asked.

"Who said I was staying in the play?" said Mike. "I just did it because of Rosalie."

The Pony Pals exchanged a glance. Was Mike going to drop out?

The Secret

Rosalie took Mike's hand. "I was scared something happened to you," she said.

Mike put his arm around Rosalie's shoulder. "Rosalie can come to the lake with us. Let's go."

"Hey, taking your sister's a drag," complained Tommy.

"We can't go to the lake," whined Rosalie. "You have to be in the play, Mike. You have to." She began to cry.

"Rosalie, stop crying," he said angrily, "or I won't take you anywhere."

"You have to be in the play because — because — " Rosalie said through her tears. " — because Daddy's coming to see it."

"What?" asked Mike, surprised.

"Daddy's coming to see you in the play," repeated Rosalie. "It was a big secret. I wasn't supposed to tell you."

Anna felt tears come to her own eyes. Mike's father left his wife and kids to move to Chicago with a girlfriend. Mike hardly ever saw his father. And Mr. Lacey *never* came back to Wiggins.

"Are you sure Dad's coming?" asked Mike.

Rosalie nodded. "He's coming to see you for one show," she explained. "Mommy's coming for the other one." Rosalie smiled through her tears. "I'm going to *both* shows."

Mike looked at Tommy. "I have got to be in this play," he said. "I can't screw up."

"Suit yourself," said Tommy coldly. "I'm not going to watch you in some kids' show."

Tommy jumped on his bike and rode in a circle around them.

"It's not just a kids' show, Tommy," commented Lulu. "It's *family entertainment.* Your mother and sister will probably come."

"Mimi and her mom and dad are coming," said Rosalie. "But they can't bring Tongo."

William and the actor who played Damien came back outside. The actor was pushing a unicycle.

"Hey, young man," William called to Tommy. "I want to talk to you."

"I got a right to be here," said Tommy. "It's a free world."

William pointed to the unicycle. "Do you think you could ride this thing?" he asked.

Tommy looked at the unicycle. "That's so *cool*," he murmured.

"How do you stay up on one wheel?" wondered Mike out loud.

"It takes practice," said the actor. "And a lot of balance."

"I want someone to ride the unicycle around town," explained William. "It's a way to get attention for the play. The rider will pass out announcements." He looked

Tommy right in the eyes. "Do you want to do it?"

Rosalie clapped her hands. "Tommy, can you do it? Can you ride on ONE wheel?"

"Sure," bragged Tommy. "It'll be easy. You gonna pay me?"

"No," answered William. "But if you learn to ride it, the unicycle is yours."

"Wow!" exclaimed Mike. "Do it, man."

Tommy spun the wheel of the unicycle. "Sure," he said. "I'll ride it."

"Let's go over to the parking lot," said the actor. "I know how to ride it. I'll teach you."

Tommy and the actor left with the unicycle.

Mike and Anna exchanged a smile. Tommy would be advertising the play. He wouldn't give Mike a hard time about being in it.

William was smiling, too. "Now," he said brightly, "we can get on with the rehearsal."

The evening of the first performance of *Magic Pony* was warm with a clear blue sky.

It was perfect weather for an outdoor performance.

The Pony Pals groomed Acorn and covered him with gold glitter. They put flowers in his mane. His coat glowed when they walked across the town green.

Tommy Rand rode the unicycle forward and backward in front of the library. "Hear ye, hear ye," he shouted. "The *Magic Pony* is about to begin. Come one and all. Hear ye, hear ye."

For once, Tommy didn't call the Pony Pals the Pony Pests.

Anna went into the library to put on her costume and makeup. Pam and Lulu took Acorn into the woods to wait for his part.

Mike was already in his costume. Is Mike as nervous as I am? wondered Anna.

"Did your father come?" she asked.

Mike nodded. "He's already in the audience," he said in a shaky voice. "He wanted to get a good seat. William said the show is *sold out*."

Anna looked out at the people going to

their seats in the park. She was surprised to see Rema Baxter handing out programs. It seemed like everyone in Wiggins was either helping with the play or watching it.

Anna saw her mother and father in the first row with Lulu's grandmother. Pam's parents and the Crandal twins were in the row behind them.

It's a sold-out crowd, she thought. The butterflies in her stomach fluttered.

I am Kalandra, Anna told herself. I am a sick princess who is looking for a magic pony.

A few minutes later, Anna-as-Kalandra walked out the back door of the library and the first performance of *Magic Pony* began.

As scene followed scene, Anna remembered all her lines and performed them brilliantly.

It was time for Kalandra's scene with the Magic Pony. Anna-as-Kalandra came out of the woods, sat on the rock, and sang the lullaby. Suddenly, a golden pony walked toward her. A magic pony that could heal her.

The Magic Pony bowed to her.

When the play was over, the audience broke into applause.

The cast lined up in front of the tree house. Anna and Acorn joined the line. The cast held hands to bow. Anna gave Acorn a signal. He bowed with them.

The applauding crowd rose to their feet and cheered. Anna saw her friends and family in the first two rows.

Anna put her arms around Acorn's neck and hugged him. Gold glitter covered her cheek and arms.

"You are my magic pony," Anna whispered to Acorn. "My very own magic pony."